To Amalya "Molly"

As thunder shakes her bed, scary thoughts crawl in her head.

Bangs, booms, whistles and zooms - all too loud to let our lady snooze.

With wind howling and screeching so loud, she pulls her head under the blanket to escape the sounds.

Thuds and thumps echo through the wall.

What monster exists in the hall?

The door swings open and light fills the room, a large shadow in the hallway looms.
She gathers her courage and peeks over the covers.
What horrors will she discover?

But before she can even look to the door,
"Let's go frolicking Molly!" she hears with a roar.

And there in the doorway barking in from the hall, stands her stuffed Hippopotamus but it's not like him at all.

Stiff yet plushy is
Hippo on the shelf, but
here in the doorway it
isn't himself. Lovely eyes,
an expressive face.
Is Hippo alive?
How did he get to this
place?

With hesitation, Molly climbs from her bed. A hippo ride does seem better, she thinks in her head.

But my parents say that while riding is fun, we must wear our helmets when wheels are being spun.

So, on bicycles, tricycles, scooters, and skates, you must wear a helmet to keep yourself safe.

Hippo follows Molly down the hall and into the garage where the shelves are so tall.

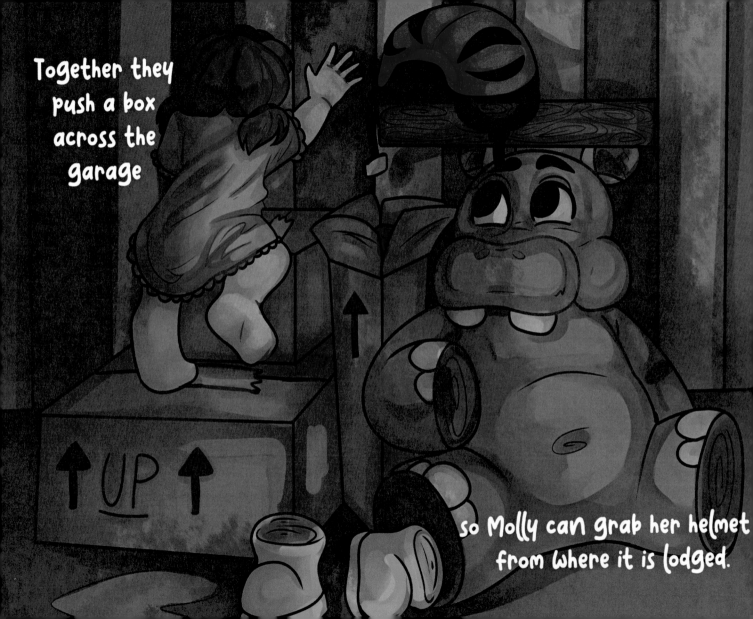

"Shall we go out and see what's in store?"
The thunder rumbles, rocking Molly to her core.
"But the sound is so scary. I can not go out"
"You must face your fears," Hippo responds in a shout.

Out they went into the storm.
Thankfully, Molly grabs her
jacket so she can stay warm.

Now outside the house rain is
coming down. But Molly did
not feel the need to frown.

Back inside they went to take off their wet clothes and get under a blanket to warm up their toes.